minnie 'n me

WISH YOU WERE HERE

BY Naomi McMillan

ILLUSTRATED BY Vaccaro Associates

Disney
PRESS

NEW YORK

Minnie 'n Me: Wish You Were Here
is published by Disney Press,
a subsidiary of The Walt Disney Company,
500 South Buena Vista Street,
Burbank, California 91521.
The story and art herein are copyright © 1991
The Walt Disney Company.
No part of this book may be printed
or reproduced in any manner whatsoever,
whether mechanical or electronic,
without the written permission of the publisher.
The stories, characters or incidents
in this publication are entirely fictional.

Published by Disney Press
114 Fifth Avenue
New York, New York 10011

Printed in the U.S.A.

ISBN 1-56282-036-2

8 7 6 5 4 3 2 1

This book is dedicated to

 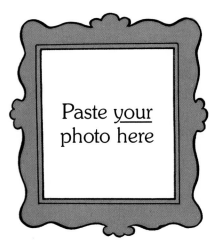

Paste your
photo here

"Now remember," said Minnie. "We're going to wear out our matching sweaters with the pink hearts."

"Right," agreed Daisy. "I'll bring the sandwiches. You bring the fruit and drinks."

Ever since their teacher had told them about their special Saturday trip to the planetarium, Minnie and Daisy could talk about nothing else.

"Only one week to go!" said Minnie.

"I can hardly wait!" said Daisy.

For the whole next week Minnie and Daisy thought of new things to bring and to wear. Minnie and Daisy loved going on trips together. And planning them was half the fun.

But the day before the trip, Daisy looked really sad.
On the way to school she hardly said a word.
"What's the matter?" asked Minnie.

• 7 •

"I can't go on the trip. My grandma is coming tomorrow," said Daisy.

"Oh, no!" cried Minnie. "I don't want to go without you."

At recess Minnie and Daisy didn't want to play any games. They just sat on the swings and talked.

"I'll still make your lunch," said Daisy.

"That's okay," said Minnie. "I can make a peanut butter sandwich. But who will I sit next to on the bus? What if I get lost at the planetarium? Will anyone know I'm gone?"

Minnie had never worried about these things before. She usually had Daisy with her where ever she went.

That night Minnie had trouble falling asleep. Maybe I shouldn't go on the trip at all, she thought. "No, that's silly," she said to herself. "I really <u>do</u> want to go."

So Minnie took out her diary and wrote, "I am going to the planetarium tomorrow. Without Daisy. But maybe it won't be so bad to go alone."

Then Minnie slept soundly for the rest of the night.

The next morning Minnie walked to school, where
the bus was waiting.

She looked around. "Maybe Daisy's grandma
couldn't come. Maybe Daisy will show up after all,"
thought Minnie. But Daisy did not come.

When Minnie got on the bus she saw an empty seat
next to her classmate, Lisa. Minnie was surprised
Susie wasn't with her. They always sat together.
"Is it okay if I sit here?" Minnie asked Lisa.
"Sure," said Lisa.

As the bus bounced along, Minnie and Lisa talked about their favorite things to do. "I like baking, reading, and ballet," said Minnie.

"I like ballet, too!" said Lisa. "I have a class once a week."

"So do I!" said Minnie. "Do you want to sit together at the planetarium?"

"Okay," said Lisa.

But when they piled out of the bus, Lisa found
someone waiting for her.

"Susie!" cried Lisa, running to her friend. "Where
were you?"

"I was late," said Susie. "Mom had to drive me here."

Lisa and Susie were so glad to see each other, they forgot all about Minnie and wandered off without her. "Bye," said Minnie softly.

Minnie followed her class to the auditorium. "I
shouldn't have come," she thought. "Not without Daisy."

Once everyone was seated, the lights dimmed. The room filled with the stars of the Milky Way and all the planets. Minnie stared at the rings around Saturn and soon all she could think about were the spinning planets and the twinkling lights all around her.

"Ooh," sighed Minnie. The star clusters were so beautiful! They reminded her of when she and Daisy tried to count the stars one night last summer. They ended up giggling so hard they kept losing track.

Minnie turned to the empty seat beside her. "Daisy would love this," she thought.

When the lights went up during intermission, the teacher led everyone to the planetarium gift shop.

Minnie saw something she just had to have. She paid for it, then returned to the auditorium with her class.

After the show there was a picnic on the lawn in front of the planetarium. Minnie was about to sit down when someone tapped her on the shoulder. It was Lisa. Susie was next to her.

"Hi! Do you want to eat lunch with us? We're going to sit under that tree," said Lisa.

"Okay," answered Minnie. She was glad she wasn't going to have to eat alone. "I like Lisa and Susie," thought Minnie. "I bet Daisy would like them, too. Oh, Daisy, I wish you were here."

Daisy was at home with her grandma. They had
gone out for lunch. Then they went shopping. Now
they were going to bake cookies.

"There's a special kind I'd like to make, Grandma.
Okay?" asked Daisy.

"Of course," agreed Grandma. And they got to
work.

Daisy had fun mixing and measuring. I know how much Minnie likes to bake, too, she thought. Oh, Minnie, I wish you were here.

As soon as she got home Minnie went over to
Daisy's house. They both jumped up and down,
talking at the same time about the day.

Then Minnie said, "I have something for you."
She gave Daisy the package from the gift shop.

"I love it!" said Daisy, as Minnie held up a beautiful star-shaped pin. "Now I have something for you."

"Peanut butter cookies!" said Minnie. "Thank you! They're my favorite."

"I had a really good time today," said Minnie. "But there was one thing I kept thinking."

And Daisy said, "I bet I was thinking the same thing."

"Wish you were here!" said the two friends together. And they gave each other a great, big hug.